Children's

The WARLORD'S PUZZLE

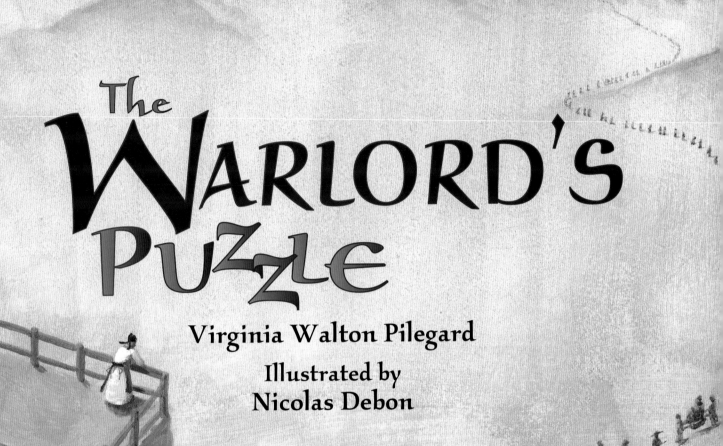

The Warlord's Puzzle

Virginia Walton Pilegard

Illustrated by
Nicolas Debon

PELICAN PUBLISHING COMPANY
Gretna 2000

To Mrs. Walton, Mr. Weyand,
Mr. Eckland, Mrs. King,
and all teachers
who help students solve life's puzzles

Copyright © 2000
By Virginia Walton Pilegard

Illustrations copyright © 2000
By Pelican Publishing Company, Inc.

The word "Pelican" and the depiction of a pelican are trademarks of Pelican Publishing Company, Inc., and are registered in the U.S. Patent and Trademark Office.

c.1

Library of Congress Cataloging-in-Publication Data

Pilegard, Virginia Walton.
    The warlord's puzzle / by Virginia Walton Pilegard ; illustrated by Nicolas Debon.
        p.   cm.
    Summary: Hoping to avoid punishment for breaking a beautiful tile that was his gift to a Chinese warlord, an artist suggests that the warlord hold a contest to see if anyone can mend it.
    ISBN 1-56554-495-1 (hc : alk. paper)
    [1. China—Fiction. 2. Tangrams—Fiction. 3. Puzzles—Fiction.] I. Debon, Nicolas, ill. II. Title.
PZ7.P6283 War 2000
[E]—dc21
                                                                                    99-054656

Printed in Hong Kong
Published by Pelican Publishing Company, Inc.
1000 Burmaster Street, Gretna, Louisiana 70053

THE WARLORD'S PUZZLE

Many years ago in China there lived a fierce
warlord. He was strong and brave and
ruled over many people.

One day an artist, knowing that the warlord loved beautiful things, brought a blue tile to the palace. There was no tile like it in all of China. It was the rare blue of a winter sky when dark storm clouds part.

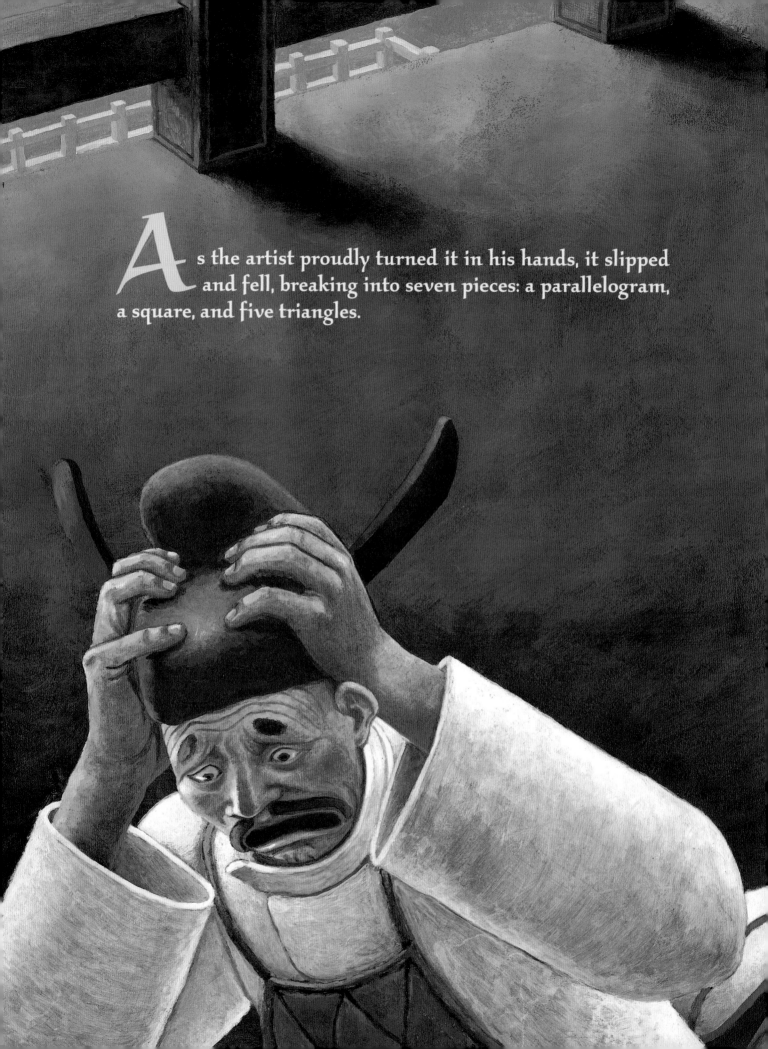

As the artist proudly turned it in his hands, it slipped and fell, breaking into seven pieces: a parallelogram, a square, and five triangles.

"MEND IT,"

ordered the warlord.

With trembling hands, the artist tried in vain to fit the pieces together. "The man who destroyed such beauty deserves my worst punishment," the warlord said.

The frightened artist hurried to suggest a solution. "Perhaps, most Honorable Master, you could announce a contest and offer a prize for the one who puts the tile back together."

The warlord rubbed his chin.

The artist held his breath.

At last the warlord said,

"Anyone who can solve the puzzle of the tile will be given a great treasure and brought to live in my palace."

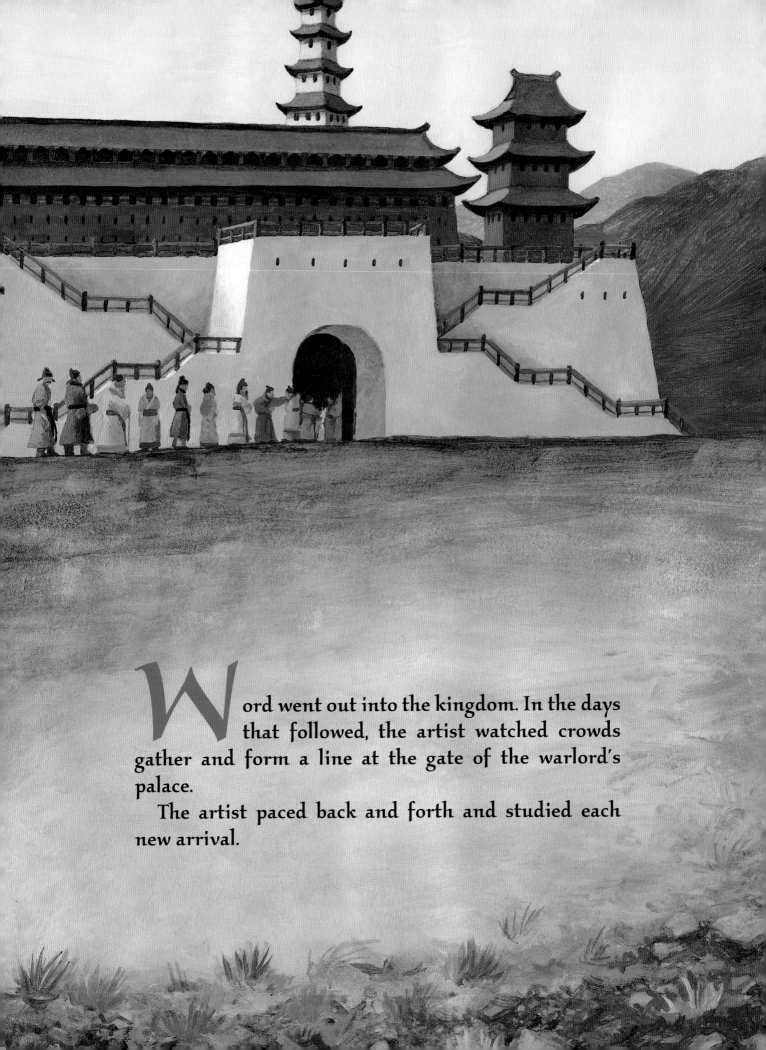

Word went out into the kingdom. In the days that followed, the artist watched crowds gather and form a line at the gate of the warlord's palace.

The artist paced back and forth and studied each new arrival.

At the end of the line a haughty scholar with a wispy beard leaned on an ivory-handled walking stick. Behind him stood a round-faced monk dressed in a yellow robe. Surely, thought the artist, one of these two fine men will solve the puzzle.

The end of the line had reached the river, where a poor peasant and his son fished for their supper.

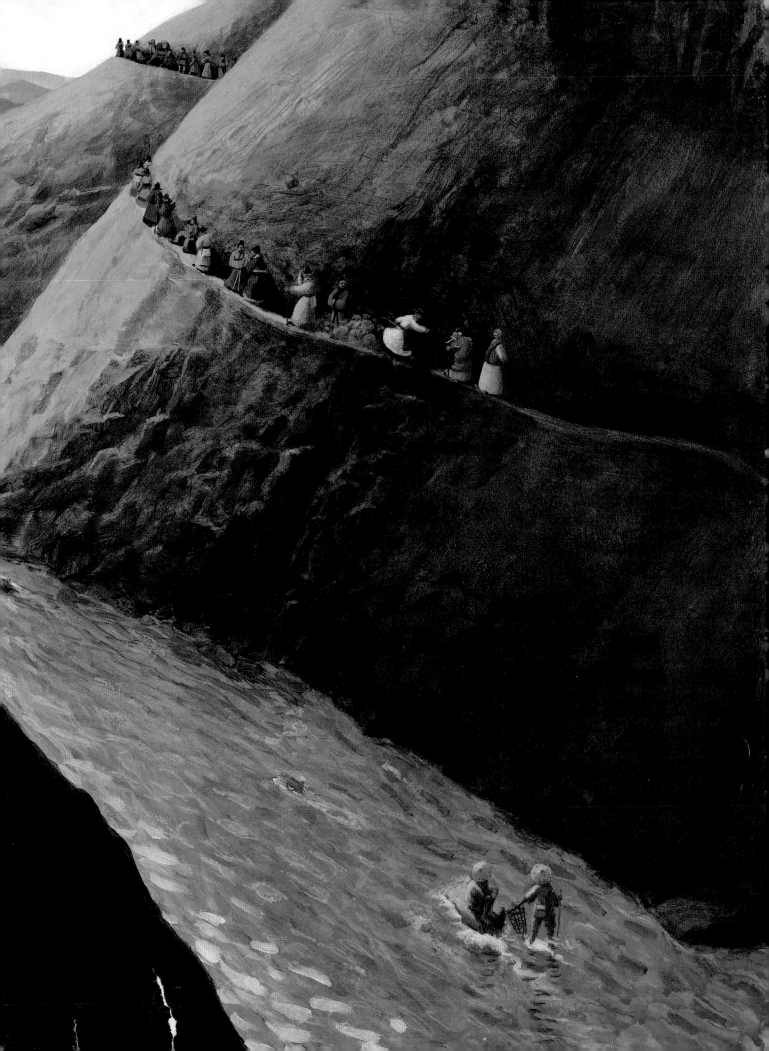

"What are all you hon-orable people doing?" asked the peasant.

"We are waiting to solve a puzzle for the warlord," answered the scholar. "A poor peasant such as you should not even ask."

"**f**orgive my most humble and poor self for asking," said the peasant, "but why do you fine and important people wait so long to solve this puzzle?"

"The one who solves the puzzle will win a fine treasure and be brought to live in the warlord's palace," the monk replied, with a kind smile.

The people standing in line were making much noise and kicking little clods down the bank into the water.

"We may as well go home," the peasant said to his son.

"Most Honorable Father," the boy whispered in a voice so soft the artist could barely hear, "you are a poor man and a peasant, but you are very clever. Why don't you join the line of people and try to solve the war-lord's puzzle?"

"I am sure your son would like to see inside the palace," the artist said.

"The excitement may make my son forget his empty stomach. There will be no fish for his supper," remarked the peasant. And so, the little boy and his father joined the others.

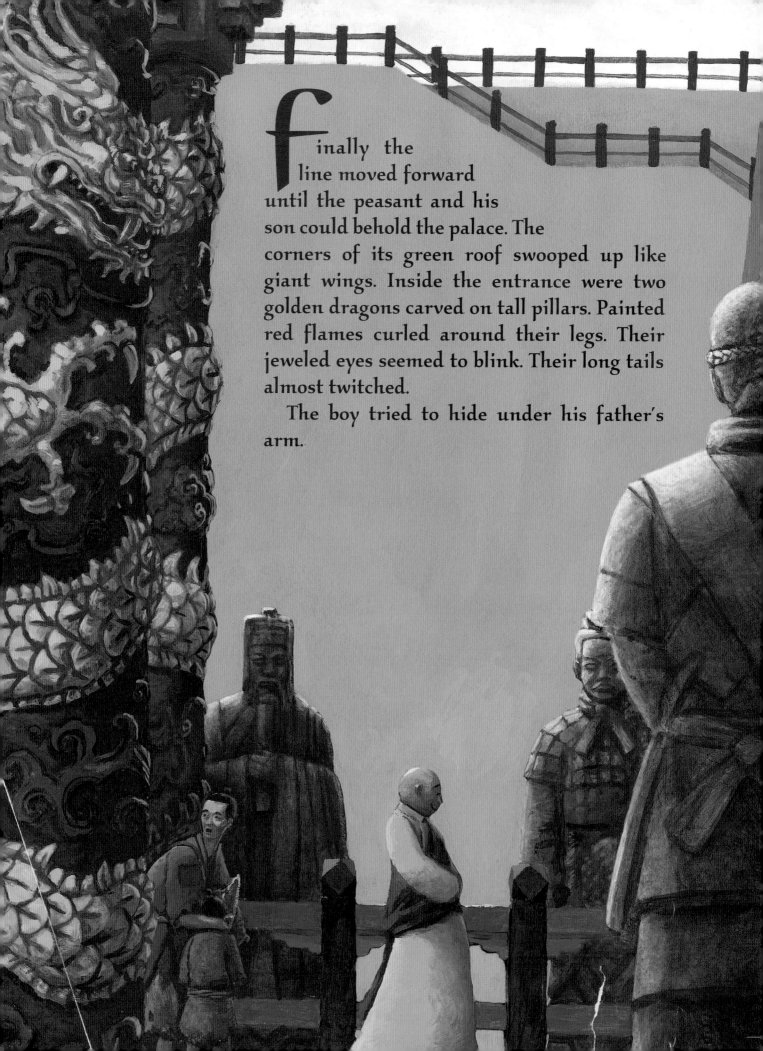

finally the
line moved forward
until the peasant and his
son could behold the palace. The
corners of its green roof swooped up like
giant wings. Inside the entrance were two
golden dragons carved on tall pillars. Painted
red flames curled around their legs. Their
jeweled eyes seemed to blink. Their long tails
almost twitched.

The boy tried to hide under his father's
arm.

The artist noticed that all of the people in the line cowered when they stopped beside a frightening statue of the warlord on his horse, even the haughty scholar.

The warlord was seated in his banquet hall on a high-backed, gilded chair. When he saw the artist, he scowled. "I think you have wasted my time, artist. I should send these bothersome people away and send you to your well-deserved punishment."

The artist's glance darted to the floor where the pieces of the broken tile lay in a hopeless jumble. "Oh please, Honorable Master, look at these fine people. Surely one of them will mend your beautiful gift."

The scholar straightened his stooped shoulders and made a short speech about the many books he had read and the important teachers he had studied under.

He pushed the pieces this way and that with his walking stick until the warlord grunted with disgust and ordered him away.

The artist trembled. He pulled the sleeve of the monk's robe. The monk knelt. With his eyes closed, he stacked the pieces, largest on the bottom.

"This one will succeed," said the artist, risking a peek at the warlord's stern face.

"A riddle in clay," said the monk, looking up with a grin. "Some riddles are meant to have no answer."

"Enough!" roared the warlord. "Artist, these two offend me more than all the rest. They will share your punishment."

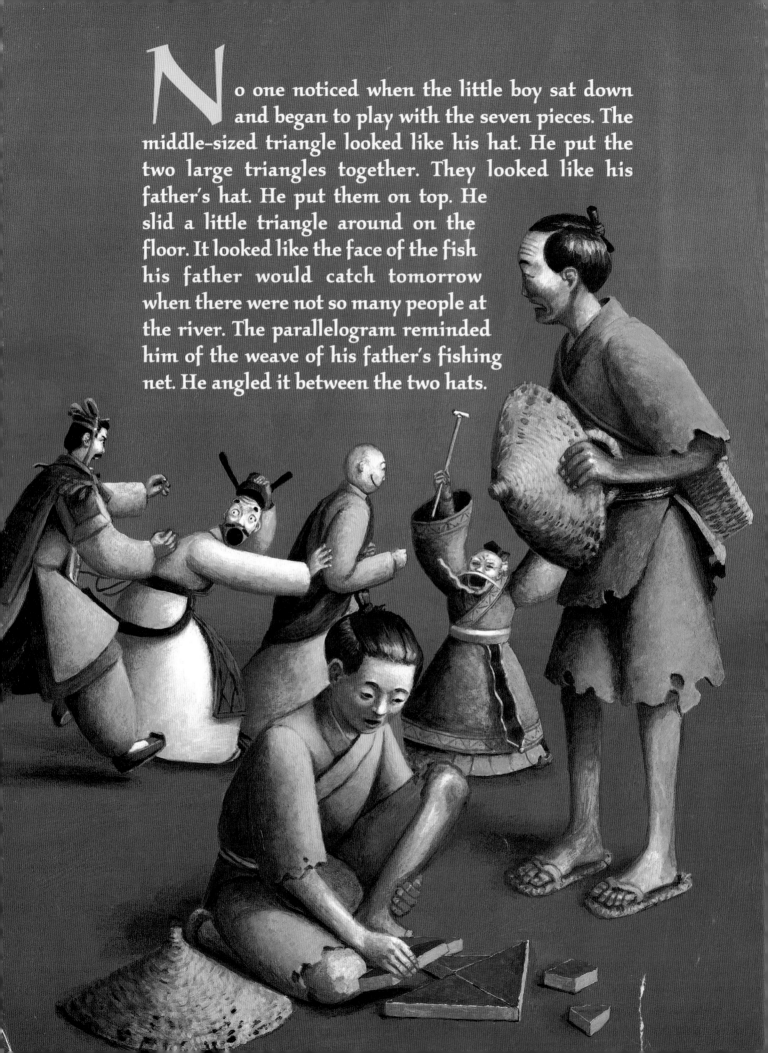

No one noticed when the little boy sat down and began to play with the seven pieces. The middle-sized triangle looked like his hat. He put the two large triangles together. They looked like his father's hat. He put them on top. He slid a little triangle around on the floor. It looked like the face of the fish his father would catch tomorrow when there were not so many people at the river. The parallelogram reminded him of the weave of his father's fishing net. He angled it between the two hats.

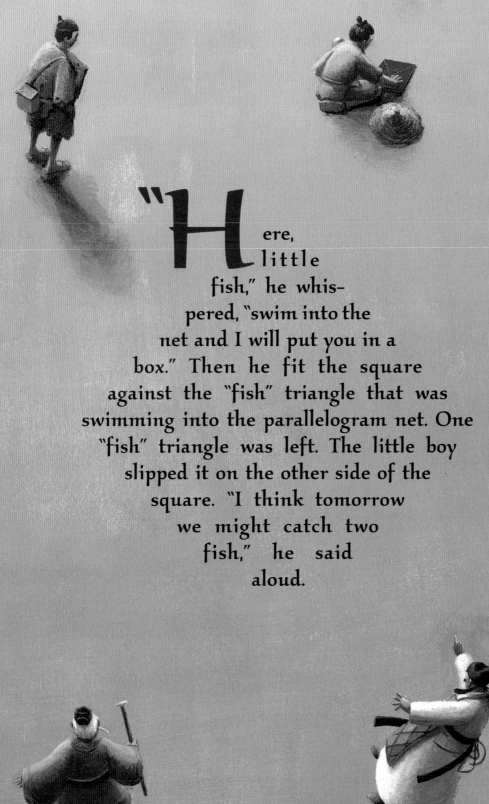

"Here, little fish," he whispered, "swim into the net and I will put you in a box." Then he fit the square against the "fish" triangle that was swimming into the parallelogram net. One "fish" triangle was left. The little boy slipped it on the other side of the square. "I think tomorrow we might catch two fish," he said aloud.

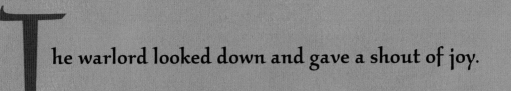

The warlord looked down and gave a shout of joy.

Weak with relief, the artist hugged the peasant and his son.

The fierce warlord was as good as his word. He gave the boy a treasure of carved jade and inlaid boxes and moved him and his family into the palace. The artist lived to make many more beautiful tiles, which he always held most carefully.

Y ou may have guessed that the warlord's puzzle was a tangram. It was said to have originated in China during the T'ang dynasty when an artist dropped a square tile that broke into seven pieces. French general Napoleon I, writers Lewis Carroll and Edgar Allan Poe, and Pres. Teddy Roosevelt are among those who have been fascinated with its deceptive simplicity.

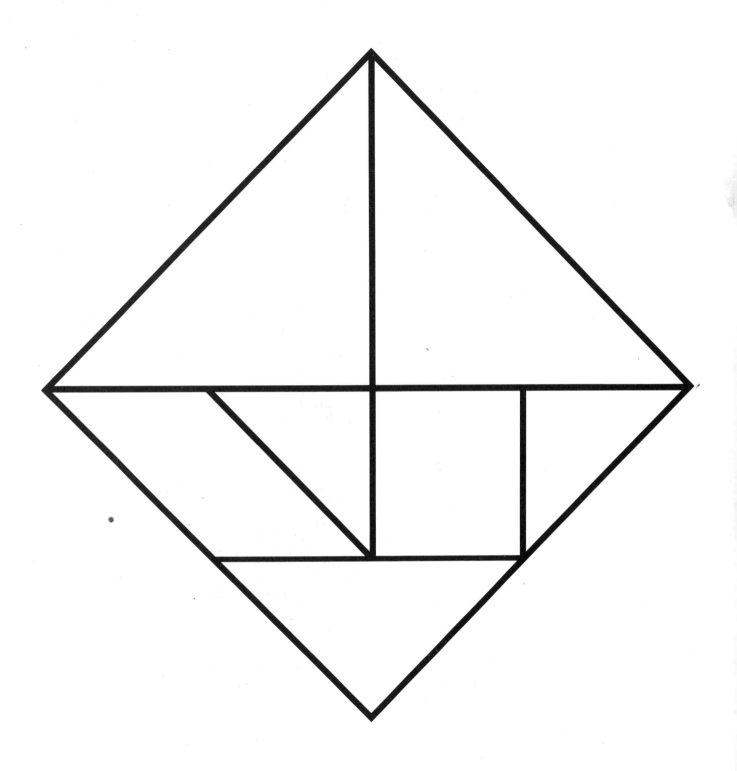

You can make your own tangram puzzle. Just trace these shapes onto cardboard and cut out, or cut out the shapes from this page.